# BLYTHE'S BIG ADVENTURE

## A Panorama Sticker Storybook

Adapted by Ruth Koeppel

Reader's
Digest
Children's Books®

New York, New York • Montréal, Québec • Bath, United Kingdom

Usually Blythe Baxter loved taking car rides with her dad. Roger was a pilot, so he was away a lot. But today Blythe sat in the backseat, hiding behind her sketchbook.

"I'm excited about our new apartment in the city," Roger said. "Aren't you looking forward to your new school?"

"NSM," Blythe told him. "Not so much."

"You love adventures. Maybe you can think of this as a great adventure," her dad suggested.

Roger parked behind their moving truck.

Blythe peered out the car window. "We're moving into a pet shop?" she asked.

"Hey, guys, it's the top apartment," Roger called out to the moving men.

At the doorway, Blythe found herself face-to-face with identical twin girls.

"I'm Whittany Biskit."

"And I'm, like, Brittany Biskit." The twins looked
Blythe up and down.

"Do you want to go shopping with us?' asked Whittany.

"We'll…like…let you," Brittany added.

Blythe got the feeling that the twins weren't very nice.

"No, thanks," she said quickly, starting up the steps.
"I better go unpack."

Blythe tried to get excited about her new life as she set up her room.

"Maybe if I keep telling myself this is an adventure, it'll come true," Blythe told herself. She used the end of her guitar to pry open her window. But the window turned out to be a panel covering a dumbwaiter.

Blythe climbed inside the dumbwaiter's car. "Now, this is an adventure!" she said with a smile.

Slowly, Blythe lowered herself down the dusty shaft. "Achoo!" she sneezed, letting go of the rope for just a second. "Whoaaa…" The car fell to the bottom of the shaft.

When the dust cleared, Blythe was lying on the floor.
Suddenly, she heard voices.

"Who is she?" asked Vinnie.

"I hope she's not hurt," said Penny Ling.

"She seems sturdy," said Russell, poking Blythe's shoulder.

Blythe's eyes fluttered open. She sat up quickly.

"You're a porcupine!" she gasped.

"Hedgehog, actually," said Russell.

"Oh, good, she can sit up," said Minka.

Blythe pointed at Minka. "Talking
monkey!" she shrieked.

Blythe introduced herself to the pets, and learned all of their names.

Zoe

Pepper

Vinnie

Sunil

Penny Ling

Minka

Russell

Suddenly, a woman appeared. "Why, hello, dear. I'm the Littlest Pet Shop's owner, Mrs. Twombly. Welcome!"

"Wake up, Blythe," a voice said.

Blythe yawned. "Morning, Dad. You won't believe the dream I had. I met a talking porcupine!" Then she opened her eyes. "Aaaaagh! It wasn't a dream!"

It was Russell. "Actually, I'm a hedgehog," he reminded her. "Blythe, we need your help. Littlest Pet Shop is in trouble!"

Meanwhile, Zoe was flipping through Blythe's sketchbook. She held up one design—a sparkly, fashionable outfit.

"That looks pretty good on you," said Blythe.

Roger knocked on the door. "Blythe, are you up?" he called out.

Blythe hustled the pets into the dumbwaiter. "Today I start at my new school. Down you go," she said, grabbing the dumbwaiter's rope.

But Russell tried to stop her. As she lowered them down the shaft he called, "Blythe, if you don't help us, the shop will close, and we'll have to go to day camp at Largest-Ever Pet Shop, the biggest, coldest, unfriendliest pet shop in the city!"

The pets met in the day camp area to discuss the fate of Littlest Pet Shop.

Zoe struck a dramatic pose. "The only thing to do is hold a benefit show with great singers—like me!" she said.

"Excuse me, but a comedy show is gonna pack 'em in," Pepper piped up. "Why did the rubber chicken cross the road? Because he wanted to stretch his legs!"

"Two words: Dance-athon," said Vinnie, tripping over his own feet and taking Pepper down with him.

"Maybe Blythe can make Mrs. Twombly's problems…disappear!" Sunil said, like a magician. He threw down a smoke bomb, scorching himself by accident.

"Ugh!" Russell groaned in frustration. "We're trying to solve a problem and all any of you can do is show off!"

"Quiet, everybody," Zoe hushed the other pets.
"Something's going on up front with Blythe and Mrs. Twombly."

"Wow, Blythe looks really excited about something," said
Minka edging closer to the window.

"I love designing clothes," Blythe explained. "But I never
thought of designing them for pets…"

"Oh, pet clothes are so popular! Go on," Mrs. Twombly
urged Blythe excitedly.

"If we could put on a fashion show and get all the
day camp pets to model my designs," Blythe continued,
"people would come for the show and remember how
much they love the shop."

"Let's do it!" Mrs. Twombly agreed.

The pets ran over and jumped on Blythe, barking and
squealing with joy.

After school, Blythe got started. The pets were there to
help. Minka helped Blythe pin up her sketches on the walls
of her room. Vinnie brought in a bolt of fabric and dropped
it in front of Sunil, who pushed it across the bedroom floor.

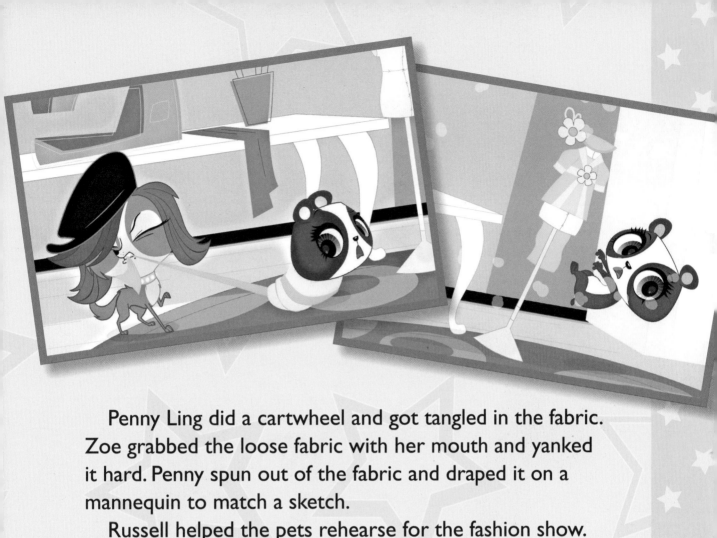

Penny Ling did a cartwheel and got tangled in the fabric. Zoe grabbed the loose fabric with her mouth and yanked it hard. Penny spun out of the fabric and draped it on a mannequin to match a sketch.

Russell helped the pets rehearse for the fashion show. One by one, they came out of Blythe's closet, practicing their runway walk.

Outside the building, Minka hung by her tail from
a tree and taped a flyer to the tree's trunk. Then she
jumped down to join Blythe and the other pets as they
hung the posters all around the neighborhood.

The flyer read: TODAY! PET FASHION SHOW! TO SAVE LITTLEST PET SHOP FROM CLOSING ITS DOORS FOREVER! Exclusive pet fashions by Blythe Style. Available only at Littlest Pet Shop!

The Biskit twins watched as Blythe set up for the show.

"This new girl is getting a lot of attention!" said Brittany.

"Uh, yeah, and we've got to do something to stop it," said Whittany.

By the end of the day, a stage had been erected in front of the shop. The fashion show was good to go. It was time for the pets to hit the catwalk.

Mrs. Twombly peeked out from behind the curtains. "Oh, my, that's some crowd out there! Those fliers of yours sure did the trick."

While the crowd was distracted, Whittany and Brittany climbed onto the catwalk disguised as cats, carrying buckets of chocolate icing and kitty litter to dump on the stage.

Mrs. Twombly stood on stage before the crowd. "The first ever Littlest Pet Shop fashion show is about to begin!" announced Mrs. Twombly. "I'd like to introduce *Blythe Style*, our exclusive new line of pet clothes!"

"Okay, everyone, you're gonna be great," Blythe told the pets. "Just remember, be yourselves."

The pets strutted out on stage. The crowd went wild when Penny Ling, Minka, Pepper, Vinnie, and Sunil pranced down the runway.

Russell caught sight of the twins and realized they were up to no good.

Just as the twins were about to pour the kitty litter and chocolate onto the stage, Russell curled up into a ball and rolled toward them.

"Ahhh! A porcupine!" the twins cried.

"I'm a hedgehog!" Russell called out as the twins fell backward off the catwalk and got tangled in some ropes.

Blythe and the pets burst into laughter.

Embarrassed, the twins ran off the stage, leaving Blythe to take a bow. The show was a success—and Littlest Pet Shop was saved!